This book belongs to:

....

T0371150

Based on the episode "Paddington and the Magic Trick" by Jon Foster and James Lamont

Adapted by Megan Roth

First published under the title *The Magic Trick* in the USA by HarperFestival, an imprint of HarperCollins in 2020.
Published in this edition in the United Kingdom by HarperCollins *Children's Books* in 2024.
HarperCollins *Children's Books* is a division of
HarperCollins*Publishers* Ltd
1 London Bridge Street
London SE1 9GF

www.harpercollins.co.uk

HarperCollins*Publishers*
Macken House, 39/40 Mayor Street Upper
Dublin 1, D01 C9W8, Ireland

1 3 5 7 9 10 8 6 4 2

ISBN: 978-0-00-862166-7

Printed in Malaysia

Conditions of Sale
This book is sold subject to the condition that it shall not, by way of trade or otherwise, be lent, re-sold, hired
out or otherwise circulated without the publisher's prior consent in any form, binding or cover other than that in which
it is published and without a similar condition including this condition being imposed on the subsequent purchaser.
No part of this publication may be reproduced, stored in a retrieval system or transmitted in any form or by any means, electronic,
mechanical, photocopying, recording or otherwise, without the prior permission of HarperCollins*Publishers* Ltd.

All rights reserved

Based on the Paddington novels written and created by Michael Bond

PADDINGTON™ and PADDINGTON BEAR™ © Paddington and Company/STUDIOCANAL S.A.S. 2024
Paddington Bear™ and Paddington™ and PB™ are trademarks of Paddington and Company Limited
Licensed on behalf of STUDIOCANAL S.A.S. by Copyrights Group

This book is produced from independently certified FSC™ paper
to ensure responsible forest management.

For more information visit: www.harpercollins.co.uk/green

The Adventures of
Paddington™

Abracadabra!

HARPERCOLLINS
CHILDREN'S BOOKS

Dear Aunt Lucy,

You have always told me the magic word is "please", but this week I learned a new magic word: "Abracadabra!" And it is a very magical word indeed! It all began in Mr Gruber's shop . . .

"Behold!" said Mr Gruber, placing a rather ordinary ball underneath a rather ordinary cup. "And now for the magic word . . ." he said, raising his wand.

"Please!" shouted Paddington.

"The *other* magic word," Mr Gruber said.

"Thank you?" Paddington tried.

"Oh, you are such a polite bear," Mr Gruber said. "No, the magic word I mean is . . .

Abracadabra!"

Mr Gruber tapped the top of the cup with his wand.

TINK!

When he lifted the cup, the ball had vanished!

Paddington was so amazed he fell off his seat. "That was incredible, Mr Gruber! The ball was there and then it was gone. You're **a magician!**"

"I wonder," Paddington continued, "if it's not too much bother, would you show that trick to the Browns? I'm sure they would love it!"

"How would you like to show them the trick yourself?" Mr Gruber asked.

"I'd love to . . . but I'm not a magician," Paddington said sadly.

"We can fix that," Mr Gruber said, opening an old chest filled with costumes. He found the perfect magician's outfit and a box of magic tricks for Paddington.

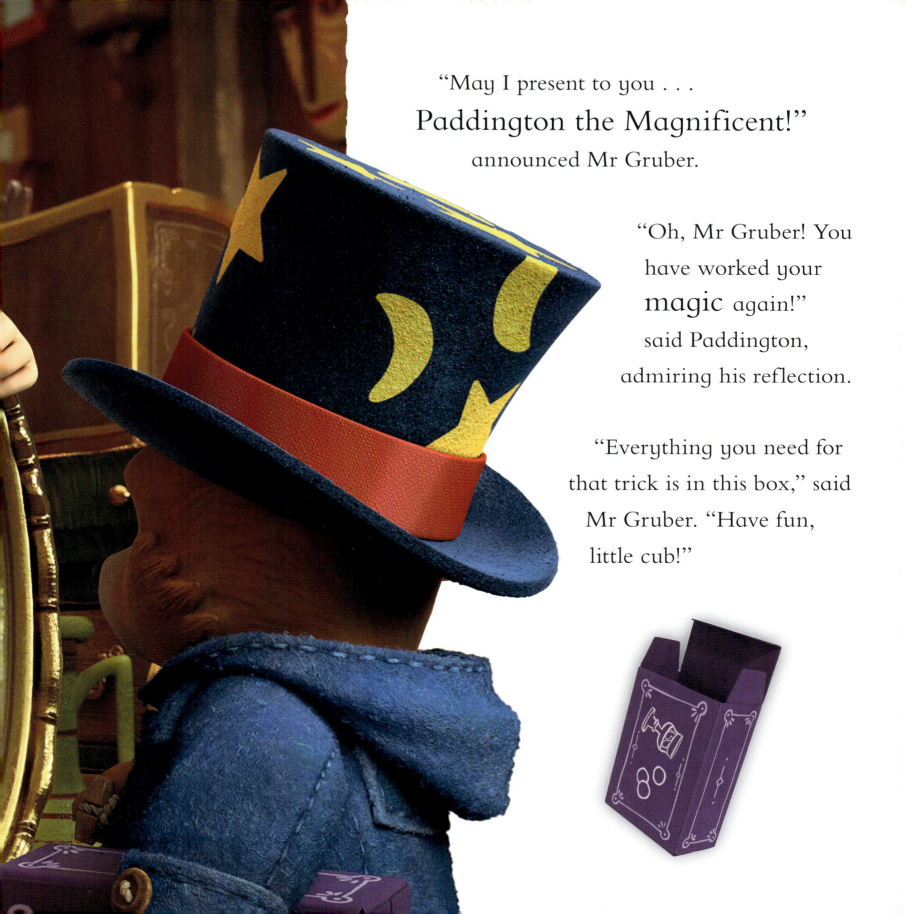

"May I present to you . . .
Paddington the Magnificent!"
announced Mr Gruber.

"Oh, Mr Gruber! You
have worked your
magic again!"
said Paddington,
admiring his reflection.

"Everything you need for
that trick is in this box," said
Mr Gruber. "Have fun,
little cub!"

Back in the Browns' living room, Paddington
prepared to show Mr and Mrs Brown, Jonathan
and Judy his magic trick. They were very excited!

"Ladies and gentlemen, boys and girls," Paddington began in his very best magician voice. "Prepare to be amazed as you welcome to the stage Paddington the Magnificent!"

"An ordinary ball," Paddington said. "An ordinary cup. I place the ball beneath the cup, say the magic word . . ."

"Thank you!" shouted Jonathan.

"Hocus pocus!" shouted Mr Brown.

"Please don't be silly, Mr Brown. That *isn't* a word," said Paddington.

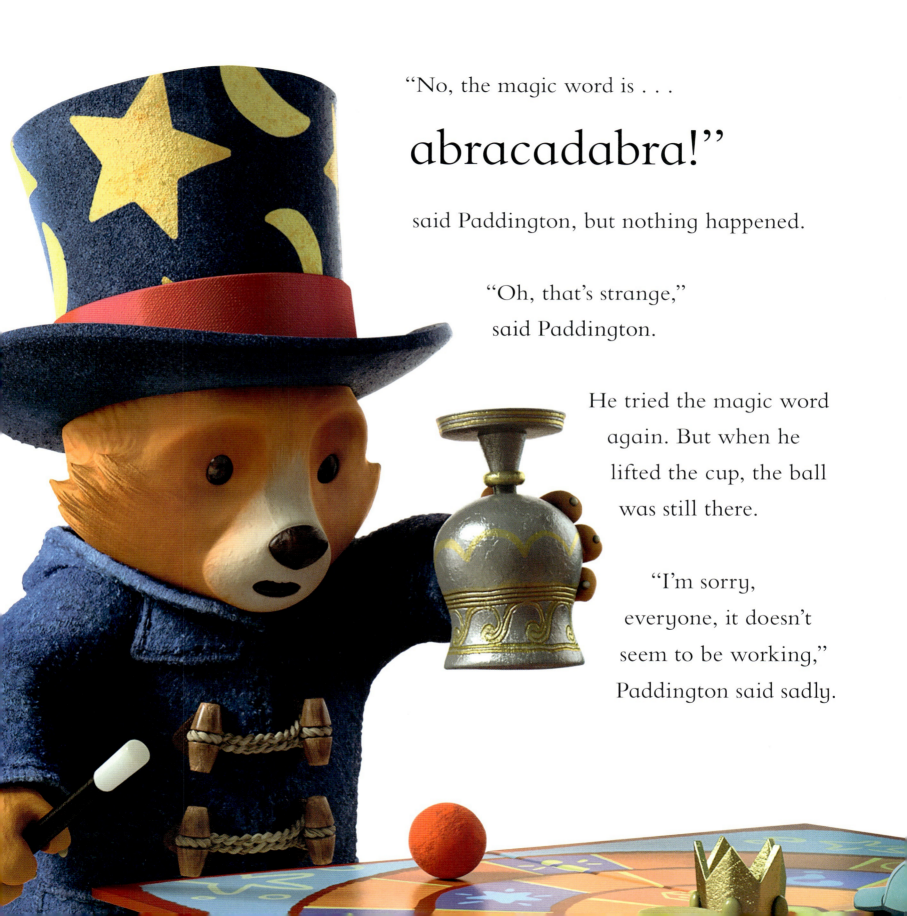

"No, the magic word is . . .

abracadabra!"

said Paddington, but nothing happened.

"Oh, that's strange,"
said Paddington.

He tried the magic word
again. But when he
lifted the cup, the ball
was still there.

"I'm sorry,
everyone, it doesn't
seem to be working,"
Paddington said sadly.

Paddington walked back to the shop and explained to Mr Gruber what had happened.

"That's odd. Did you follow these instructions?" Mr Gruber asked, showing him the little piece of paper.

"I didn't know there were instructions," Paddington replied.

"It's my fault, Paddington. I should have been clearer. You see, magic tricks have to be practised," Mr Gruber explained. "Look here. There is a **secret button** on the cup. When you tap the button with the wand, this secret compartment slides shut and hides the ball."

"So, you are saying magic isn't real," Paddington said disappointedly.

"Oh no, magic is *very* real, Paddington," Mr Gruber said. "But the magic isn't in the trick. It's in the happiness it brings to others. Would you still like to try and be Paddington the Magnificent?"

"Yes, I would like that very much," Paddington said, ready to try again.

So Paddington went back to his room with an even bigger box of magic tricks. He even tried to master new tricks!

Paddington practised again and again and again. He practised so much that eventually he needed a little rest.

ZZZZZZZZ!

But when his alarm went off the next day, Paddington the Magnificent was ready for his big show!

TA DA!

The Browns sat down to watch again.

"Prepare to be more amazed than you have ever been amazed before, by the one, the only, **Paddington the Magnificent!**" he said.

And this time,
Paddington was **ready!**

He magically pulled
a bunch of flowers out
of his hat and gave
them to Mrs Brown.

Paddington even
made Pigeonton
appear out of thin air!

He broke
Mr Brown's
watch and then
fixed it with
magic, before
making Judy
disappear and
reappear through
a magical door.

"And now, for my final trick," Paddington began. "I shall make this ordinary ball vanish from beneath this ordinary cup . . .

Abracadabra!"

He waved his wand, lifted the cup, and the ball vanished!

CLAP! CLAP! CLAP! CLAP!

It worked!

The Browns clapped and cheered.

"But where did it go?" Jonathan asked.

"Normally a magician would never reveal his secrets," Paddington replied. "But Mr Gruber told me that real magic is the happiness it brings to others. Since it would make you happy to know, let me tell you . . ."

But the ball wasn't in the cup, Aunt Lucy! And it wasn't on the table,
or the floor, or up my sleeve, or under my hat, or even behind Jonathan's
ear. In fact, we searched everywhere. Perhaps magic is real after all . . .

Love from,
Paddington the Magnificent